BETWEEN NOW AND MARRIAGE

*A Christian Woman's Guide to
Navigating Her Single Season*

Erica S. Howard

Published in United States.
Gen Wealth Publishing.

For more information, contact us at promisetomarriage@gmail.com.

ISBN 978-0-578-78880-7
First Edition October 2020

Committed to helping women heal from their past, discover their passion, and pursue their purpose.

Dedicated to

The woman who wants to be married but desires the purpose God has planned for her even more. And to the woman who wants to find fulfillment within herself, so that she can become one with her purpose partner.

ACKNOWLEDGMENTS

First, I give thanks to the Father,
who put this book in my spirit to write.

Thank you to those who have supported me and contributed to my growth in one way or another. Although I kept this project close to my heart, your voices were the ones I heard, telling me to press forward.

Thank you to the life lessons and experiences that I've had to endure that make this book so personal. There were nights I cried and days I worried, *"What next?"* But through it all, God was with me, ordering my steps. I'm so in awe of where those encounters have led me and hope they can also push you to achieve greatness.

For my future husband and children, just know that even now, this was done with you in mind.

Forever Grateful.

TABLE OF CONTENTS

Preface   1

Chapter 1 Growing with God   5

Chapter 2 Dealing with Heart Issues & Healing from
Past Trauma   13

Chapter 3 Your Quest for Purpose   23

Chapter 4 Navigating Your Career   37

Chapter 5 Authentically You   49

Chapter 6 Facing Your Finances   59

Preface

The **#1 complaint** I hear from women is, *"God, I'm ready for my husband, where is he!?" Or "I'm lonely; if I had someone, then everything would be complete."* Or something similar, but you get the point. I'll be honest; I've made these same statements a time or two myself. But it wasn't until I got further along in my single season that I started to appreciate and be truthful with myself. I wasn't ready to be in a relationship. I wasn't finished with my inner WORK, and I hadn't built the type of relationship I desired to have with God. I wanted a husband more then I wanted to know God. It wasn't until I started working on myself that I began to discover hobbies I enjoyed, figured out what my purpose really was, and was honest enough with myself to admit that I didn't bring enough to the table.

I had a job in my career field, a new car, and a place to stay. I paid my own bills and essentially was able to provide for myself. But was that enough? When I started to peel back the layers, I discovered some truths about myself that I wasn't happy with. It was in that moment that I wanted to change. Yes, I had a good job, but it was only good because I could pay my bills. The position I had wasn't fulfilling. It wasn't something that inspired me. It didn't fuel my passion, and I knew I didn't want to be there long term. It made me tired because it didn't challenge me mentally. I felt like I had to conform to their standards, and it made me question my morals. So, how could I consider that a good job?

I had a new car, but I was paying almost $500 a month because my interest rate was so high. My credit was the best because I defaulted on my student loans, which caused me to pay an extremely high-interest rate. But hey, it was a new car, right? I was living in a 2-bedroom duplex, but I was still renting. I could have been living in a condo for the amount I was paying in rent every month. I could pay my monthly bills, but I didn't have money to set aside for savings, and I wasn't able to travel the way I wanted.

This journey helped me change my mindset about many areas of my life, and ultimately, I started to want more. As a result, I started making changes in my life to make that possible. This book is intended to help you to discover who you are in Christ so that when the time is right, you'll fully understand the role that you play in your relationship. How can God send you someone if you aren't first who He needs you to be? That's how you fall into the same cycles, date the same types of men, and ultimately continue to be stuck in the same place. We are all worthy of finding a love so great that we'll understand why the wait took so long. Each chapter will cover different areas in your life that are worth taking a look at. The information provided is not all-inclusive, but there could be areas in your life where you need to grow. It takes the focus from finding a man and puts the focus back on God, on you, and being the best verse of yourself.

Maybe God wants you to develop a closer relationship with Him. Perhaps you need to heal from past relationships or trauma that took place in your childhood. You may need to work on your finances or discover your purpose. By examining specific areas of your life, you'll discover why you aren't able to settle for less than you deserve, and you can start to lead a life more fulfilled, whether you have someone or not. Take care of yourself first and the rest will fall into place.

There may be certain areas of your life that you may already be familiar with and other areas where you haven't even scratched the surface. Use this book as a guide to uncover areas of your life that the Lord wants to work on. Use this time to seek Him, meditate, and do the necessary work. What I've come to understand by going through the different areas of my life is that this process is like an onion. For example, you might have gone through a time where you've worked on your credit, but you can always gain additional knowledge. There may be times when you need to take a break and do some activities not provided by the book, but that is the Spirit challenging you to do so. There may be seasons when you feel the information is speaking directly to your situation. There may be situations when you become upset with yourself. But remember, it's all part of the process. This is God's way of pruning and allowing you to do the soul work needed to grow. You may never be able to master everything fully; you are perpetually a work in progress, but you can move the needle forward. Educate yourself on the foundations of YOU and the areas of your life that require work.

Say this prayer for yourself as you read through the chapters:

PRAYER FOR SELF-REFLECTION

Father,

As I contemplate the act of self-examination, I pray that your word will be the mirror that shows me to myself. I want to look at myself as you do through the eyes of truth. You have ordained this necessary act. Your word says to let every man examine himself. Therefore, in the act of obedience, I come to you. Uncover me to my own self so that I can see who I am. Whether there is sin, shortcomings, faults or imperfections, help me own up to what you reveal. Take away fear, pride, and blame so I can be face to face with what you want me to see about my true self. This way, I can prepare myself to live for not only myself but for you and others as well.

Amen.

Chapter 1
Growing with God

PRAYER FOR A DEEPER RELATIONSHIP WITH GOD

Dear Heavenly Father,

You are awesome and amazing. You are my protector and provider. I come humbly before you today and pray for your guidance and wisdom and that You will allow me to walk in Your righteousness. I thank you for always looking after my interests and teaching me to look to you for all my needs. Reveal to me deeper truths about you so that I will know you in a deeper way. I pray that I will be taken into a deeper, more meaningful relationship with You. I pray that I am open to the plans that you would have for my life and help me become attentive to Your voice. Allow me to grow in faith and take me to new heights, where I can experience the overflow of Your grace, mercy, and especially Your love. Father, guide my steps and remove every negative thought that keeps me from receiving all that You would have for me. I thank You in advance for fulfilling all my needs.

I pray these things in Jesus' name.
Amen!

101.   Maturing in Your Relationship With God

God's desire for each one of us is that we draw closer to Him through prayers and devotions, so that He may be able to use us to advance the kingdom. He wants us to willingly accept all that He would desire for us on our own. He doesn't expect us to be perfect, but He does want us to give Him the power to make us whole. He wants us to be able to hear His voice so that He may direct our next steps. But if we aren't aware of His love for us, then we are less likely to understand the authority He has given us. Not only do we open ourselves up to being hurt, but we can't help others find a relationship with Him.

There are times when God needs to remove all the distractions from your life so that you have no excuse for getting to know Him more intimately. But instead of thinking He wants to take something from you, He wants to give you something greater. He wants to give you Himself!

Your single season is your time to grow closer to God, learn His voice, and discover the purpose He has for your life. Take the time to develop a history with God. This is an opportunity to be consistent—consistent in reading your Bible, praying, and hearing clearly from Him. Learn not to just pray when you are in need. Pray for His guidance and direction in all areas of your life. Pray and pray daily. Be so confident in your ability to hear His voice that you praise Him for the times your plans don't work out.

Ultimately, you can become the person He needs you to be so that you can glorify His Kingdom. This is often around the same time He introduces you to your PURPOSE Partner (Hubby). You are demonstrating that you have made Him a priority and won't make marriage an idol. But for Him to do all these wonderful things, He has to rid your life, mind, body, and spirit of things that prevent you from delivering your very best. In the upcoming chapters, I will go over some areas in your life that you may need to work on in order to start being the best version of yourself.

Reading God's Word

To mature as a believer, you must first learn God's word. When you allow the word of God to resonate and become a part of you, His voice becomes easier to identify. Every story in the Bible was written specifically with you and your personal situations in mind. You will never find out what God has to say about you if you don't invest your time reading it daily.

For those of you who are just beginning, start by taking small steps every day and work your way up to being fully immersed in His presence. Just 5-15 minutes a day can change your outlook on life. You may also start to notice yourself being more patient, becoming more empathetic, and wanting to uplift those around you.

God wants you to mature as a believer, and you'll know when you start to grow, when you become more consistent in your prayer time and the reading of His word. You will then begin to grow in prayer, and your prayer life will start to develop. Once you start becoming obedient, you will feel convicted about the choices you make. You will develop a relationship with Him outside of seeing Him as the Father. He can now be a friend. You're not coming to

Him out of a moment of needing help but you're coming from a position of wanting Him because He is enough. You are now developing history with God.

How Marriage Changes Your Relationship with God

In your single season, this is the only time when it's just you and Him. You will then be able to take that history into your future marriage so that you and your spouse can continue your relationship with God as the center. When you get married, your desires are going to be split between God and your husband. By having a relationship with God before you get married, you can go to Him in prayer for your husband and circumstances that happen in your marriage.

102.   Having a Servant Heart

How are you serving those who can't do anything for you?

A true servant is humble and does not expect to get acknowledgment for their acts of service. They do not brag about what they've done, but they look for opportunities to be helpful because they understand the gifts they've been given and have a desire to help others. This concept is one of the truest forms of maturing in Christ because it requires you to do something that many people don't want to do. It is denying yourself and putting someone else's needs before yours, and one of the key principles of being a disciple is to serve.

How to Start Serving

If you aren't already serving, you can begin the process by looking at the relationships around you and ask yourself, *"How can you serve others?"* How can you serve your family, friends, coworkers, church, and community? There are projects that they need help with now. Start by committing to one task or one hour a week, then build from there. Be open to help when needed, not just when you feel like it. Because if you don't know how to be selfless now, you probably don't need to be married.

Serving Those You Don't Know

But the true test will come when you have to serve those you don't know—when you aren't able to receive from that person. All you can do is give. This can often be seen when people are in public.

How do they treat their servers? How do they treat customer service reps? How do they treat those that they consider being in a lower position than them? That's when you get a glimpse of their heart. To be able to set aside your feelings and emotions and consider someone other than yourself is maturity.

Serve like Jesus

Jesus came not to be served but to serve, and He asked us to do the same. What Jesus did was a symbol of His love and having a true servant heart means we humble ourselves in love and service to others. Then you will find fulfillment in the day-to-day tasks without the need to get anything from others. You can learn to put serving into practice daily so that when you are married, you will value what it means to be selfless.

103.   Fasting

Fasting is a way of focusing your mind and body for a spiritual purpose. Fasting is giving up food or something else for some time to focus your thoughts on God, and food is one of the ways we've kept ourselves comfortable. We tend to think of fasting as going without food. But we can fast from almost anything. If we love music and decide to miss a concert to spend time with God, that is fasting. He doesn't give us a specific amount of time to fast. He gives us the choice to make those decisions for ourselves. It's just one way of telling God that your priority, at that moment, is to be connected to Him.

Although there are different types of fasts, many people read the Bible, pray, worship, or all the above, while fasting. It's a way for you to regain control, detox your body, and build up resistance. It's a way to get to God quickly. This is about drawing near to God and getting clarity like never before. Make sure you set expectations for what you want God to do in your life.

If prayer is extending faith for things unseen, fasting is letting go of all that is seen and temporary. Fasting helps in expressing, deepening, and confirming the thought that we are ready to sacrifice anything, even ourselves, to attain what we seek for the kingdom of God. This implies that there is something in the act of fasting that elevates you, bringing you into a closer relationship with God.

Preparing for the Fast

Here are some things to consider as you prepare for fasting:

- Spend time meditating on God's Word before and during the fast.
- Turn to Scripture
- Pray and confess your sins
- Keep it secret
- Prepare your body
- Seek Reflection

As you set your intention for your fast, do so for a reason mentioned or modeled in the Bible. Below are ten primary purposes for fasting mentioned in the scripture:

1. To express repentance and a return to God (1 Samuel 7:6) - This fast helps you express repentance over your sins and shows your commitment to returning to the path of obedience.

2. To express grief (1 Samuel 31:13) - Expressing grief is one of the primary reasons for fasting.

3. To humble oneself before God (1 Kings 21:27 – 29) - Fasting is not humility before God, but an expression of humility.

4. To seek deliverance or protection (2 Chronicles 20:3 – 4) - Fasting in the Old Testament was to seek deliverance from enemies or circumstances. In Scripture, this fast commonly occurs with other believers.

5. To seek God's guidance (Judges 20:26) - Fasting to seek God's guidance makes you more open to His presence.

6. To strengthen prayer (Ezra 8:23) - Several events in the Old Testament connect fasting to prayer, especially intercessory prayer.

7. To express concern for the work of God (Nehemiah 1:3 – 4) - Fasting can be a physical sign of your concern over the work God is doing in your life.

8. To minister to the needs of others (Isaiah 58:3 – 7) - You can use the time normally spent eating to minister to others.

9. To overcome temptation (Matthew 4:1 – 11) - Fasting can help you focus when you are struggling with temptation.

10. To express love and worship for God (Luke 2:37) - Fasting can show that what you desire most, you worship.

104. Make Me Over

What Does It Mean to Be Made Whole?

When people think of wholeness, then think of physical health, sickness, or mental wellness. Wholeness, however, is a matter of completion within the body, soul, and spirit. It is living in such a way that all aspects of our lives are aligned so that it provides peace from the inside out.

When God corrects you, He does so with the purpose of putting us back together so that we might be made complete within Him. First, we must recognize that we have three aspects to our being— spirit, soul, and body.

Body - the way in which we relate to our environment.
Soul - our mind, will, and emotions. The soul is your way of relating to other people. You choose with your will and mind how you will act in the world and towards other people.
Spirit - your inner person. With the spirit, you can relate to God.

Being in Relationship with God

To be whole, you must have a cleansed spirit and a good relationship with God. The Bible says that when you receive Jesus Christ as your personal Savior, the Holy Spirit comes to reside within you. When the Holy Spirit lives in you, you are given a feeling of His presence, an awareness of Him, and a living relationship with Him. That relationship allows you to talk to Him and Him to speak to you. You are open in new ways to understanding the Word of God and receiving guidance and direction from the Holy Spirit. You are also more sensitive to sin and the conviction of the Holy Spirit.

The Spirit Within You

The rebellion that keeps you from being whole is a rebellion of the spirit. The problems that stand as barriers to you being made whole are ultimately things in the spirit. Among them are:

- lack of trust
- pride
- greed
- anger
- hatred
- bitterness
- fear

For the Lord to bring you to wholeness, He must deal with the areas of your life that keep you from being whole. They are what separates you from the fullness of God's desire for you.

Submitting to God

Your role in times of brokenness is to submit not only to what God desires to do in your life but also to His timetable. Wholeness may not come quickly or easily, but it is worth the wait! God will reveal His plan and purpose to you step by step. You are called to trust Him day-by-day. When God is at work in your spirit, you must recognize that the most valuable aspect of your life is strengthened, developed, and refined.

You must also recognize that no matter how long you struggle, your time is brief compared to the larger goal. What is happening on the inside of you has the potential to last and remain unchanged. If you submit your life to God, He is at work creating something better and everlasting. He is putting things back into their proper order: the spirit first, the soul second, the physical third. Your purpose is to bring Him glory. Your greatest glory lies not in what you can achieve and do on your own, but in what you allow the Lord to do in your life so that you bring Him glory.

BIBLE VERSES

1 Thessalonians 5:23
Now may the God of peace himself sanctify you completely, and may your whole spirit and soul and body be kept blameless at the coming of our Lord Jesus Christ.

1 Peter 2:24
He himself bore our sins in his body on the tree, that we might die to sin and live to righteousness. By his wounds you have been healed.

Matthew 17:20-22
He said to them, "Because of your little faith. For truly, I say to you, if you have faith like a grain of mustard seed, you will say to this mountain, 'Move from here to there,' and it will move, and nothing will be impossible for you." As they were gathering in Galilee, Jesus said to them, "The Son of Man is about to be delivered into the hands of men,

2 Chronicles 7:14
If my people who are called by my name humble themselves, and pray and seek my face and turn from their wicked ways, then I will hear from heaven and will forgive their sin and heal their land.

Hebrews 6:1-2
Therefore let us move beyond the elementary teachings about Christ and be taken forward to maturity, not laying again the foundation of repentance from acts that lead to death, and of faith in God, instruction about cleansing rites, the laying of hands, the resurrection of the dead, and eternal judgement.

Titus 2:11-13
For the grace of God that brings salvation has appeared to all men, teaching us that, denying ungodliness and worldly lusts, we should live soberly, righteously, and godly in the present age.

Mark 10:45
For even the Son of Man did not come to be served, but to serve, and to give his life as a ransom for many.

Chapter 2
Dealing with Heart Issues & Healing from Past Trauma

PRAYER FOR HEALING

Lord, I release everything to You that has tried to hold me back. Please, forgive me for the times I have said and done things thoughtlessly. Also, allow me to forgive those that have wronged me. I release the past. I release bitterness. I release failures and missed opportunities. Instead, I embrace Your grace and power to boldly move forward into the blessing You have for me in Jesus' name.

Amen.

201.   Trauma and Triggers

Many of us come into adulthood, having experienced some sort of trauma. For some of us, that experience was never acknowledged or healed. You may not even be aware that you experienced trauma to even begin the healing process. Your single season is the best time to take inventory of your past and identify the parts of your life that need to be restored, without necessarily having to worry about providing for another person. This process may require professional counseling, a period of solitude where you reflect on your personal experiences or addressing your feeling with people you feel have wronged you. Whatever the situation, this is often where most people struggle. It's hard work; it leaves you emotionally vulnerable, but it can also bring you the peace you deeply desire.

Types of Trauma

Trauma is defined as a deeply distressing or disturbing experience. It can be further broken down into two different categories—primary and secondary trauma.

Primary or Big T trauma are events that include serious injuries, natural disasters, sexual violence, sexual identity, the sudden death of a loved one, or life-threatening experiences. Being close to someone who has experienced a primary trauma such as a significant other, child, or close friend, can also show symptoms of trauma even if you did not experience the situation directly.

Secondary or Little t trauma can also have a significant impact on one's life. These situations may be even more stressful because they can last an extended period without having a foreseeable end date. They can include long-term medical illnesses, emotional abuse, loss of a job, death of a pet, change in the living environment, bullying or harassment, and loss of significant relationships, to name a few.

The Effects of Trauma

Although people dealing with a traumatic event experience the effects differently, there is a difference between not dealing with your feelings and healing from the experience. Depending on the person, the effects of trauma can also lead to PTSD.

Common Symptoms You May Experience from Trauma

1. Disturbing thoughts and memories—often occurring when confronted with something that reminds you of the traumatic event.
2. Hypervigilance—more cautious and concerned with your surroundings after a traumatic event.
3. Hyperarousal—more stressed and anxious after a traumatic event. These feelings keep you aware and able to react to a dangerous situation.
4. Feeling Unsafe—places or situations where you once felt safe may now be frightening if you're reminded of the traumatic event.

It's also important to know that just because you have these symptoms, it doesn't mean you have PTSD. PTSD can't be diagnosed, until at least, 30 days after a traumatic event since these symptoms can decrease over time.

202.   Soul Ties

You might be asking yourself what a soul tie is. A soul tie occurs when your soul (your mind, will, and emotions) become attached to another person and can be either a good or bad thing.

Examples of Good Soul Ties

The bond between a mother and a child is a soul tie. God designed the family so that parents and children could be tied to each other through a loving relationship.

The relationship between a husband and his wife is another example of a healthy soul tie. When a man and a woman get married, God has joined them together, and the two become one flesh.

Examples of Bad Soul Ties

You were in a relationship with a man who abused you. You really loved him, but no longer felt safe when you were with him. You try to move on, but you can't get him out of your mind and considering going back.

You were bullied a lot when you were a kid. As an adult, people no longer bully you, but you still find yourself not being able to open up to people emotionally. You continue to replay those moments in your head when you were bullied. You may have forgiven those who wronged you, but you will still suffer from the damage that was caused.

Why Soul Ties Keep You Bound

Soul ties can be formed with people you like, but they can also be developed with people you don't like, such as those who have abused, done you wrong, or left you. The circumstance of your current relationship won't matter since it's with a specific person. The soul tie will exist until it is broken. It keeps you thinking about the person all the time, and it keeps them thinking about you. It keeps you from moving on, even if you want to be free.

How To Break Soul Ties

PRAY. The blood of Jesus cleanses and washes us from all evil things. If you'd like to break an ungodly soul tie off your life, it's important to pray out loud, use the name of the person or people who have wronged you, and clap to symbolize the breaking of the soul tie.

Repeat this prayer

Father God, You paid the price with Your own blood for me to be free in every way. I plead the blood of Jesus over every unholy soul tie attached to or from me to any other person. And in the name of Jesus, with His blood, I (CLAP) BREAK every unholy soul tie right now. So, let every part of me that has been attached to someone else return to me; I receive Your gift of freedom. And let every part of anyone else that has been attached to me be broken off and return to them, right now, in the name of Jesus. I choose to be completely free today.

I renounce and break the soul tie in Jesus' name.

Renouncing the Soul Tie

Verbally renouncing something carries a lot of weight in the spirit. Just as vows can bind the soul, renouncing can release it. Jesus said that whatsoever you shall loose will be loosed in heaven (the heavenly or spiritual realm). You can renounce and loose yourself from an ungodly soul tie by simply speaking something like this from your heart:

"I now renounce and loose myself from any ungodly soul ties formed between myself and (the person's name)_____, and I break these ungodly soul ties in Jesus' name."

If you prayed that prayer, then Jesus just broke the unholy soul ties off your life. You will likely feel different after that prayer. If you feel suddenly separated from those people, that is a VERY good sign! That is what freedom feels like. It feels whole and healthy just between you and Jesus. You should feel whole and complete in Jesus alone.

What Happens Next?

If you prayed this prayer to break soul ties, be prepared that the person(s) with whom you had the ungodly soul tie may also feel the disconnect within your relationship. They may suddenly sense that you have broken free from their control or influence. And they may not like it. They will likely try to reconnect with you again. Remember that connection wasn't godly before, and it's not going to be godly now. It is a trick of the enemy to try and pull you back into bondage.

203.   Forgiving Your Parents (Let Go of Past Wounds)

Forgiving your parents or anyone else may seem insignificant, but forgiveness can add value to your life. Resentment or blame can create a cycle of suffering that leads to a negative impact on your relationships, wellbeing, and even your finances. It can prevent you from finding the love and happiness you deserve. Without healing, you will remain stuck at the age of your earliest wounds, causing you to repeat the same cycle as an adult.

Example

If you haven't forgiven your dad for missing your birthday or healed the resulting feelings of abandonment, whenever you feel triggered by a current experience, like someone forgetting to call you, the original emotion is triggered. You become your wounded ten-year-old self, and since you feel the same pain you felt then, you may react by lashing out or shutting down emotionally.

Law of Attraction

According to the Law of Attraction, you unconsciously attract people who trigger your emotional wounds. This is why a person with abandonment issues attracts potential partners who have commitment fears, not as punishment but because God wants you to heal. He will use every opportunity to bring your wounds to the forefront.

Unfortunately, this means that unhealed emotional wounds can prevent you from meeting your ideal partner, and even if you do find each other, the emotional wounds can damage your relationship.

Learn to Forgive

First, you must realize that blame, anger, and other related emotions are defensive mechanisms that protect you from reliving the moment. Since true forgiveness requires you to let go of this defense, forgiveness can make you feel vulnerable. Therefore, to forgive your parents, you must trust they won't hurt you again, but you also have to realize they're human, and it may still happen. As long as you blame or shift responsibility, you give others the power to hurt you. Therefore, the only way to prevent yourself from being hurt again is by releasing blame and taking full responsibility for every emotion you experience.

Getting to the Core Emotion

The main emotional wound is almost always unworthiness. In fact, unworthiness is the core wound of every other emotion.

All children have emotional needs that must be met to feel worthy of love and life. These needs include approval, acceptance, appreciation, understanding, validation, respect, etc. Although children require all emotional needs to be fulfilled, one emotional need almost always stands out from the rest, and because this is usually the need least met, it is the need most associated with worth.

Children naturally accept beliefs that explain why one or both parents fail to provide this need, so when a child doesn't receive approval, for example, the child naturally believes she is unworthy of approval or believes she must meet certain requirements to prove she is worthy.

You were born worthy, and there is absolutely nothing you can do to prove, improve, or disprove worth. The emotional pain associated with believing you are unworthy is because it is completely untrue!

You will attract continuous opportunities that trigger emotional pain until you pay attention and release the idea that it is responsible for the pain. False opinions caused by childhood wounds can lead to a repeated cycle of emotional pain.

Breaking the Cycle

Even the most well-intentioned parents can fail to meet their children's emotional needs, and in most cases, emotional wounds have nothing to do with parental love. Often, childhood wounds are related to parenting style or your parent's unhealed wounds or family issues, such as financial challenges, divorce, addiction, disease, mental illness, or chronic depression.

In most cases, a child's emotional wounds deepen over time, and as the child matures into adulthood, the wound matures accordingly, appearing as problematic relationships, financial concerns, career challenges, and health issues, while also making it difficult to pursue one's dreams and desires.

If you continue to crave parental approval, then you are giving your power away. Not only does this make you subject to parental judgment and criticism, but it also makes you vulnerable to manipulation through guilt and obligation. You won't be able to heal your emotional wounds or forgive your parents as long as you blame them for making you feel powerless and unworthy. This is why self-responsibility is necessary, and the only thing that can solve your problem.

Taking Responsibility for Your Emotions

Self-responsibility means that you must own your worth and take back your power by releasing the expectation that your parents meet any of your emotional needs. This also includes accepting that you may not receive an apology, acknowledge, and need to get even. Self-responsibility means that you must own your worth. Give yourself what you need from your parents.

As your family dynamics begin to change, it creates a new foundation based on worth and self-empowerment. The foundation of this deeper connection is clear boundaries, and in fact, boundaries can take you from a helpless child to an empowered adult. Your power is only as strong as your boundaries.

Boundaries Are Key

As an adult, it is up to you to set boundaries with your parents. Initially, it might feel uncomfortable, but over time, strong boundaries can help to strengthen your relationship and allow for a deeper connection.

How Boundaries are Maintained

Effective boundaries require integrity, which means that you must backup every boundary with proper and consistent attention. This means that it's your responsibility to protect your boundaries and give clear feedback, telling your mom or dad when they are crossing or about to cross a boundary.

However, if either parent does not acknowledge your boundaries, don't be afraid to limit interactions accordingly, but let them know why so they have the necessary information to change their behavior. Most parents will eventually learn to respect boundaries and remain in your life, but only if you consistently enforce them first.

Getting The Rewards You Deserve

No matter how difficult, childhood wounds can contribute to gifts such as independence, wisdom, or compassion, and without emotional challenges, our best attributes might never have been revealed. Always remember that forgiveness is not for the person being forgiven. Forgiveness is for you.

204. Forgiving Yourself

Being able to forgive yourself requires empathy, compassion, kindness, and understanding. It also requires you to accept that forgiveness is a choice. Whether you're trying to work through a small mistake or one that impacts multiple areas of your life, the steps you need to take to forgive yourself are the same.

All of us make mistakes. As humans, we're not perfect. As painful and uncomfortable as it may feel, there are things in life that are worth enduring, and being able to move forward and forgiving yourself is one of them. Forgiveness is important to the healing process since it allows you to let go of the anger, guilt, shame, and sadness you may be feeling. Once you identify what you're feeling, give a voice to it, and accept that mistakes are going to happen. You'll begin to see how much peace forgiveness can provide.

Tips for Forgiving Yourself

Focus on Your Emotions

Before you can move forward, you need to acknowledge and process your emotions. Give yourself permission to recognize and accept your mistakes.

Acknowledge the Mistake Out Loud

If you struggle to let go, acknowledge out loud what you learned from your experience. When you give a voice to your thoughts and emotions, you may be able to let go of some of the responsibility.

Have a Conversation with Your Inner Self

Journaling can help you understand your inner voice and develop self-compassion. This can help you identify thought patterns and allow you the opportunity to forgive yourself.

Take Your Advice

Often, it's easier to tell someone else what to do than to take our advice. If you're having a difficult time working through this in your head, it can help to role-play with your friend. Ask them to take on your mistake. They will tell you what happened and how they are struggling to forgive themselves. You get to be the advice-giver and practice telling your friend how to move on.

Get Clear About What You Want

If the mistake you made hurt another person, you need to determine the best course of action. Do you want to talk to this person and apologize? Is it necessary to reconcile with them and make amends?

Quit Reliving the Moment

It's human nature to spend time and energy replaying our mistakes. While some processing is important, going over what happened repeatedly is unhealthy and won't allow you to forgive yourself.

Show Kindness and Compassion

If your immediate reaction to a negative situation is to criticize yourself, it's time to show yourself some grace. The only way to begin the journey to forgiveness is to be kind and compassionate with yourself. This takes time, patience, and a reminder that you're worthy of forgiveness.

Think of Each Mistake as a Learning Experience

Remind yourself that you did the best you could with the information you had at the time, and that will help you forgive yourself and move on.

Seek Professional Help

If you continue to struggle forgiving yourself, you may want to take the next step and speak with a professional.

BIBLE VERSES

Matthew 6:14-15
For if you forgive other people when they sin against you, your heavenly Father will also forgive you. But if you do not forgive others their sins, your Father will not forgive your sins.

1 Corinthians 1:10
I appeal to you, brothers and sisters, in the name of our Lord Jesus Christ, that all of you agree with one another in what you say and that there be no divisions among you, but that you be perfectly united in mind and thought.

Luke 12:7
Why, even the hairs of your head are all numbered. Fear not; you are of more value than many sparrows.

Isaiah 43:4
Since you are precious and honored in my sight, and because I love you, I will give people in exchange for you, nations in exchange for your life.

Chapter 3
Your Quest for Purpose

PRAYER FOR PURPOSE DISCOVERY

Father, I know that you have a plan for each one of our lives. I understand that Your desire for your children is to know You first. I thank you that You have a perfect plan and purpose for my life. Help me to fulfill all that You would have me do in my life. Father, I want to be obedient to Your voice as I seek to carry out Your purpose for my life. Use every gift and every talent that You have graciously provided to me to glorify Your Holy name.

This I ask in the name of Jesus,
Amen.

301.   Discovering your purpose

Have you ever thought, *"What was I created to do?" "What is my purpose?"* or *"What value do I add to the world?"* Well, if this sounds like something you've either thought or said, then you're not alone. God's desire for your life is to bring you clarity and to help guide you to your purpose.

Discovering your purpose can be difficult, and you may need help in determining where God wants to lead you. If you want to live a life fulfilled, happy, content, and experience inner peace, you must first learn how your gifts are aligned with your passion and life's purpose. Without a life purpose to act as a guide, you will have a hard time fulfilling the desires that God has for your life.

"Your purpose explains what you are doing with your life. Your vision explains how you are living your purpose. Your goals enable you to realize your vision." - Bob Proctor

Getting Clarity

For some of you, your purpose and passion in life are obvious and clear. You were born with a unique set of talents, and through consistent practice, you developed your talents into skills. Though, for some, it's not as easy to identify their passion.

I feel strongly that each of you was born into this life with several potential paths to achieving your purpose. There may not be any "one" job that is just perfect for you. But there are probably many opportunities in several different areas of interest that will make you feel like you're where you belong. Fortunately for you, the people around you might be able to also give you some perspective. There's a good chance you're already walking in your passion and purpose without even realizing it.

Exploring Things That Come Naturally to You

You were all created with a deep and meaningful purpose that you have to discover in order to create a life that serves God. You can begin to discover your passion or purpose by exploring two things: What do you love to do? And what comes easily to you? Of course, it takes work to develop your talents, but it should feel natural. Although it may take time to learn how to master these skills, you should enjoy the process. Work is required, but suffering for it shouldn't be. If you are struggling and suffering, you are probably not living in purpose.

Follow the Holy Spirit

The Holy Spirit that lives within you can help you get from where you are in life to where you want to be. All you have to do is allow it to lead you and decide where you want to go by clarifying your vision. By locking in your destination through goal setting, affirmations, and visualization, start taking the actions that will move you in the right direction. With every picture you visualize, the Holy Spirit is "downloading" your future destination. Every time you express a preference for something, you are expressing an intention. All these images and thoughts are guiding you to receive your purpose.

Moving in your Purpose

If you don't interrupt the process of identifying your purpose with negative thoughts, doubts, and fears, the Holy Spirit will continue to unfold the next steps along your journey as you move forward. God wants you to do great things, so it's only natural that your vision seems too big to conquer or even frightens you. Once you clarify and stay focused, the exact steps will continue to appear in the form of dreams, new ideas, and increased opportunities.

Be Clear About Your Life Purpose

Once you are clear about what you want, resources will show up right when you need them. The things that bring you the greatest joy align with your purpose and will get you to where you want to be. When you present your goals to the Lord, you will be surprised by what He delivers. This is where miracles truly happen.

Ask the Right Questions

Take some time to think honestly and openly about where you currently are in your life and what you want to do with it. What is your financial status? How are your relationships going? How is your health? And so on...Next, think about where you would like to be. If your life were perfect right now, what would it look like? What kind of job would you have, and where would you be living? By continually doing this exercise, your subconscious mind will help navigate you where you want to be.

Conduct a Passion Test

The Passion Test, created by Chris and Janet Attwood, is a simple process. You start by filling in the blank 15 times for the following statement: "When my life is ideal, I am ____." The word(s) you choose to fill in the blank must be a verb.

Once you've created 15 statements, you identify the top five choices. To do this, you compare statements #1 and #2 to identify the most important. Take the winner of that comparison and decide whether it's more or less important than statement #3.

Then take the winner of that comparison and decide whether it's more or less important than statement #4, and so on until you've identified the passion that is most meaningful to you.

Repeat the process with the remaining 14 statements to identify your second choice. Then repeat the process until you've pinpointed your top five passions in life.

Next, create markers for each of your top five passions, so that you can look at your life and easily tell whether you are living that passion.

Once you know what your passions are and how your life will look when you are living it, you can create action plans to turn your dreams into a reality.

How Joy Can Lead to your Purpose

Another technique you can use to help you identify your purpose is to conduct a joy review. Set aside about 30 minutes and make a list of all the times you've felt the greatest joy in your life. Look for a pattern among all these times, and you can determine a lot about your life purpose from completing this joy review.

Aligning your Goals with Purpose and Passion

We're all gifted with a set of talents and interests that tell us what we're supposed to be doing. Once you know what your life purpose is, organize all of your activities around it. Everything you do should be an expression of your purpose. If an activity or goal isn't aligned with that formula, then don't do it.

Aligning with your purpose is most critical when setting professional goals. When it comes to personal goals, you have more flexibility. Nurturing yourself emotionally, physically, and spiritually will make you more energized, resilient, and motivated to live your purpose professionally.

However, don't ignore the signs that your job or career is not right for you. If you hate Monday mornings and live for the weekends, it may be a sign that it's time to follow your heart and pursue the work that inspires you.

Lean Into your Purpose

Once you have gained more clarity about your purpose, you don't need to change your life at once completely. Instead, just lean into it, gradually. Start living your purpose a little more every day and pay attention to the feedback you're receiving from others from the results you are producing, and also to how you are feeling. You've got big dreams and ambitions. Now, it's time to start acting on them while taking your life to a whole new level.

302.   Perfecting your Passion

Beyond the abilities and knowledge needed to fulfill your purpose, every discipline needs a particular set of qualities, skills, and behaviors. These are primarily soft skills that help you interact and can help to foster successful relationships with others. In some cases, hybrid skills, which are a combination of soft and hard skills, are required to get the job done.

Top 7 Professional Skills

Communication: Communication skills, in general, are important for any professional. It includes written, verbal, and nonverbal communication. However, one crucial communication skill in today's world is email. Almost every profession requires some email correspondence. Professionals need to be able to create clearly written, concise emails, using the appropriate format and tone. Other communication skills include:

- Advocating for yourself and your causes
- Asking for help or advice
- Brainstorming
- Building buy-in to an idea
- Business writing
- Dealing with difficult people
- Facilitating
- Handling office politics
- Interviewing
- Managing positive relationships
- Networking
- Persuasion
- Resume writing
- Small talk

Public Speaking: Almost every position requires some form of public speaking. While you might not be giving long presentations regularly, you will likely need to speak up during meetings, provide information to your colleagues, or speak to a group in some way. Professionals need to be capable of speaking to others clearly and presenting information effectively. The following skills are important for anyone who has to present in public:

- Articulation
- Confidence
- Creating presentation slides
- Poise
- Projection
- Receiving criticism/feedback
- Social skills

Teamwork: All professionals will work in some sort of group, whether they are working on team projects or trying to help their company achieve its vision. As a professional, you must possess the skills required to get along with others. You must be able to share responsibility with others, communicate effectively, and achieve a common goal. There are other teamwork skills professionals need:

- Conflict resolution
- Relationship building
- Team building
- Team management

Time Management: As a professional, you will be responsible for completing a variety of tasks. You'll have to draw upon organizational skills to budget your time so that you complete each task by a specific deadline without feeling overwhelmed. Timeliness might seem simple, but it is one of the most important qualities in a professional. Employees who show up on time (or, better yet, early) are often perceived to be more hardworking by their employers (even if this is not the case). You can, therefore, boost your professional reputation by showing up to work and meetings a few minutes early.

- Attention to detail
- Intrinsic motivation
- Meeting deadlines
- Project management
- Punctuality
- Self-starting

Leadership: Regardless of the role you play at an organization, leadership skills are important. Whether you're working on a team or in a management position, leading is an essential skill for a professional. Some of the skills that show your leadership abilities include:

- Accountability
- Budgeting
- Calm pressure
- Coaching
- Coordinating resources
- Decision making
- Goal setting
- Growth mindset
- Information gathering

- Influence
- Management
- Mentoring
- Meeting management
- Planning
- Politeness
- Positivity
- Prioritization

Flexibility: Most jobs require a degree of flexibility and the ability to be willing to change. It's important to be able to understand different perspectives and adjust your workflow and contributions to the company as change arises. Here are some of the skills that will enable you to show employers that you have the flexibility required for success on the job:

- Able to change your mind
- Adaptability
- Analysis
- Anger management
- Patience
- Perceptiveness
- Problem-solving

Personal Skills: Interpersonal skills are the soft skills that give individuals the ability to work with employees, managers, clients, customers, vendors, and other people they interact with. These skills and professional attributes are also necessary for successful professional networking and managing your career growth.

- Career management
- Career planning
- Competency
- Creative thinking
- Critical thinking
- Dressing professionally
- Emotional intelligence
- Enforcing boundaries
- Ethics
- Honesty
- Humility
- Integrity

- Patience
- Perceptiveness
- Perseverance
- Persistence
- Practicality
- Resilience
- Respect
- Self-awareness
- Self-confidence
- Self-management
- Self-promotion
- Self-regulation
- Stress management

303.   Mentors vs. Sponsors

Both mentors and sponsors can be valuable assets to your career growth. They can also be useful once you've identified your purpose. But what's the difference between a mentor and a sponsor? Which would best serve you in your journey? How can you find and work with mentors or sponsors? These are sincere questions that everyone should ask themselves. The answer to these questions can depend on you and what you ultimately want to achieve. We'll take a look at the difference between a mentor and a sponsor, what their roles are, how to seek them out, and what it takes to work most effectively with each one.

Defining Each Role

Mentors and sponsors serve two critical, yet separate roles that almost anyone can benefit from. Mentors serve as a guide, talking you through issues and telling you that you can do it. Sponsors serve as cheerleaders, speaking about you publicly and telling others that you can do it. You can ask someone to be your mentor; however, you cannot ask someone to be your sponsor. They typically make that decision based on your ability to perform well in your position.

Mentors

Mentors provide you with a resource to help you practice ideas, level set on issues as they arise, and gain advice on the proper way to handle various business issues. At their core, mentors can serve to help you maintain professionalism in your workplace, in the hopes of gaining career advancement opportunities.

Sponsors

Sponsors are typically senior-level people with power and influence. They believe in your talent and skills and are willing to advocate for you to get key opportunities to advance your career. The value of sponsorship is accessing key opportunities and earning promotions quickly, often even before you think you are ready. While both a mentor and sponsor may want to give you a chance, a sponsor generally has the connection to actually make it happen. There is an advance in being seen with your sponsor. They can bring you into spaces you would not be able to access on your own. You can also build credibility at a much faster rate and are recommended for projects or promotions.

Where to Find Mentors and Sponsors?

If you don't already have mentors or sponsors in your life, there are some steps you can take to find and connect with them. Think about people in your organization or field that you admire and trust. If possible, take them to coffee and ask them about their path. Find ways to connect with them and build a relationship. Actively seek mentors in your organization, through professional associations, and other networks. It's important to have multiple mentors representing diverse perspectives and experiences to gain the broadest insight and understanding. Sponsorships are valuable and not easy to attain. Sponsorships must be earned through hard work, diligence, loyalty, and proof.

Diversify your Network

Don't do your career the disservice by assuming mentors and sponsors need to look like you. While some of your greatest mentors may be women, you don't want to lose out on priceless opportunities and advice by not being open to men or other ethnicities. I recommend that you first focus on your performance, and often, the rest will find you. Consistent, high-achieving work performance always gets attention and attracts potential sponsors.

Best Practices for Working with Mentors and Sponsors

The key to forming an effective mentor relationship is not to wait for the mentor to take the lead. You can take the initiative to schedule periodic meetings and don't be discouraged if those meetings get canceled sometimes. It's not personal; it's just the nature of business. Over time, if you are consistent, the relationship will become more natural and less work will be involved. Keep in mind that these are two-way relationships and should be managed accordingly. If you want a seat at the table, you also need to bring something to it. Being able to listen and learn from both your mentors and sponsors will not only advance your career but also provide a preview about how to serve in these roles in the future. You will have the opportunity and responsibility of paying it forward.

304.   How Do you Know When You've Found Your Purpose?

The work you do feels natural

Life doesn't necessarily become easier when you find your purpose, but it just feels right. It feels like it was meant for you. Consider what type of skills, talents, and passions you bring to the table. Then, brainstorm how you might turn your passion into something meaningful to you.

You have more energy

When you find your purpose, you usually associate that with doing something that you love. The chances are that you are working harder than you've ever worked, but you are fulfilled. You wake up in the morning feeling renewed, refreshed, and ready to start your day. You sleep better at night because you love what you do and it doesn't feel like work, and finding your purpose is a lot like falling in love.

Your past has prepared you for this moment

Once you've found your purpose, you'll hear yourself say, *"I've been working for this day my whole life."* Sometimes, you'll find yourself hopping from job to job. You may also see someone owning business after business. When you find your purpose, you'll realize that all the jobs and the work you've done up until this moment have prepared you for this day. When you find the thing that you've been preparing for your whole life, you will look back and realize it wasn't a waste of your time and effort at all. You were just preparing for today.

Your purpose impacts other people

When you find your purpose, people will recognize it too because your work will impact them. You will be excited to share your purpose. You will be excited to give of yourself. You will be happy to help others explore their life's purpose. Your life is not the only one that will change. You will change the lives of everyone around you for the better.

You're Free to Take Risks

Once you've found purpose, you'll recognize your greatness. You are not scared to take risks to ensure that you will succeed, and you're willing to ask for help. You will reach out to people who once seemed unreachable, and you will emulate confidence, knowledge, and the ability to be successful.

You Meet Others with Shared Interest

You will run into people with the same or similar purpose. You will find yourself being introduced to people looking for the exact "thing" you have to offer. Your only job will be not to question it but to embrace every person aligned to your life and learn the lessons they have to teach you.

You'll Find Your Tribe

Once you find your purpose, you will notice that your network will start to seek you out. They may want your advice or need your expertise. They may just want to stand in your presence because you make them feel good about life. The reasons don't matter. You will be glad to have a network of people who have your back and want to see you succeed, and want what's best for you.

You Experience Great Peace

When you find that thing that you've been looking for all along, you will feel peace, even when you're faced with time constraints and the stress of life. When you find your purpose, you will be settled in your soul. Life will seem more peaceful because you finally know what you are supposed to be doing, and you're willing to reach back and help the next person find their purpose.

BIBLE VERSES

Proverbs 16:9
The heart of man plans his ways, but the Lord establishes his way.

Acts 26:16
But get up and stand on your feet; for this purpose I have appeared to you, to appoint you a minister and a witness not only to the things which you have seen, but also to the things in which I will appear to you;

Ephesians 1:9
He made known to us the mystery of His will, according to His kind intention which He purposed in Him

2 Corinthians 9:7
Each one must do just as he has purposed in his heart, not grudgingly or under compulsion, for God loves a cheerful giver.

Revelation 17:17
For God has put it in their hearts to execute His purpose by having a common purpose, and by giving their kingdom to the beast, until the words of God will be fulfilled.

Chapter 4
Navigating Your Career

PRAYER FOR CAREER

Dear Heavenly Father, you are awesome, amazing, and all-knowing. I thank you for continuing to keep me and your ability to protect me from myself. Father, I pray that you open doors to new opportunities. I pray that you allow me to learn the skills that lead to my success. I pray that you connect me to people who share my same love for you. I pray for Your perfect will and purpose for my life to be done. I trust in Your ability to select the best path for me because You know me better than anyone else. Keep my heart always filled with you and not worldly possessions. As You continue to bless me, I will keep on being a blessing to others, no matter what season I go through.

In your Son's holy name.
Amen.

401. Advancing in Your Career

For so long, women have identified success by the ability to climb the corporate ladder and advance their careers in a male-dominated organization. As women secure more leadership opportunities, they excel in these roles by utilizing their strengths and unique perspectives. They are unapologetically pursuing the roles, titles, and responsibilities they want, not waiting for them to be offered by colleagues. The key to their confidence is in utilizing all their resources and abilities, not just those mentioned on their resume.

Although the number of women who acquire advanced degrees continues to grow, women may continue to experience challenges in navigating to top leadership roles. Often, it rests on current female leaders to be an example to their peers and address those challenges head-on. While the circumstances may appear bleak, there is hope. Don't be afraid to take a non-traditional path to gain insight into your desired position. Taking risks, thinking outside the box, and pulling from diverse experiences, differentiate you and your experience from the crowd and could be the difference between you and the guy next to you.

The Importance of Leaving Your Comfort Zone

A study on internal hiring practices found that men will apply for a job as long as he meets 60 percent of the qualifications, while women apply only if they meet 100 percent. When I first read that article, those numbers just sounded crazy to me. But as I reflected on my own career, I thought back to all the times I didn't apply for a job because I didn't feel I measured up. Some positions were once in a lifetime opportunities. Looking back, I'm confident that my drive would have more than made up for my lack of experience.

Every woman must believe that she is not only qualified for pursuing the role but that she is worthy of the opportunity in the first place. Proving your value for a job is not solely dependent on your resume but can also be shown during the interview process. Working in HR, I know firsthand that being great on paper only gets you in the door. People want to work with people they like and are excited about the position, company, or both. They want to see the enthusiasm and someone who has a well-thought-out plan to take the role to the next level. Knowing the right questions to ask, dressing the part, and having a sense of urgency only solidify that you're the right person for the position. Do not allow self-doubt to control your ability to see your worth.

Learning to Overcome Fear

Successful leaders and entrepreneurs will all tell you that they've learned some crucial lessons throughout their careers. They did what they were afraid to do. They did what they felt they didn't have the skills for. They even did it when they weren't motivated. But regardless of how they felt, they followed through instead of just letting fear consume their personal and professional lives. And the best way to overcome fear is to acknowledge it. Recognize the fear is there but do it anyway. You don't want to miss a moment that could inspire greatness. In business, you have to get out and talk to people. Put yourself in a position to have those opportunities and show everyone just how amazing you are. If I've learned anything, it's that you will never feel that you are truly ready. You are either going to win or learn. Either way, you're preparing for what comes next.

Use your Natural Talents to Advance

Natural characteristics normally associated with women can be big differentiators as leadership qualities in the workplace. Women can help others set goals and attain them, emphasize teamwork, and invest time in training, mentoring, and personal development. Women are less likely to take sole credit for projects, lending themselves naturally to developing and advocating for others.

When women bring these qualities to lead their teams and employees, the results tend to be long-lasting. It improves employee retention, creates stronger team players, and develops the next generation of strong female role models.

Women as Leaders for Other Women

For women just entering the workforce, learn to lead them by example. Often, these women look up to you and are watching how you communicate, interact with others, and handle challenges. You may even be the measure they use to determine how successful they could be within the organization. Learn to lead while being open, supportive, and collaborative with coworkers. Look for, bond with, and become a role model that other women want to follow. You could very well be helping to shift the culture within your organization. With more awareness in the workplace, conversations are changing, cultural norms are being questioned, and the future of our companies rests in the hands of those brave enough to challenge the stereotypes.

However, if you want to continue to be considered for ongoing opportunities, you must stand your ground and demand the respect you deserve. This doesn't mean you have to be rude, but you have to speak up, take risks, and be innovative. Acknowledging the need for change is real, but more importantly are your actions, attitudes, and results in the workplace. Encourage yourself and others to use their voices to be the change they want to see.

Challenges Women Face as Leaders

Below are common issues that many female leaders face within their organizations. By creating a solution for some of the biggest challenges your company faces now, you are more prepared to discuss specific strategies when an opportunity to advance presents itself.

1. Generating Revenue

One of the biggest challenges any leader faces is increasing revenue. By researching what generates revenue within your organization now, you can find ways to continue that momentum. You can also follow industry trends, technology improvements, and get feedback from employees and customers to make recommendations based on what's happening in the market.

2. Speaking Up

It's not just enough to have a seat at the table; you must also be willing to confidently come forward, regardless of what obstacles you may face. Female leaders can fear being excluded or rejected; however, respect comes when you use your voice. Your perspective can help shape policy, the workforce, and create new strategies. Make your presence known as a leader and collaborator.

3. Building Alliances with Decision-Makers

Women need to build healthy relationships with advocates, create a strong personal brand, establish guidelines before each project, position themselves as experts in their field, and communicate effectively. Knowing how to network and the ability to find common goals helps to make this challenge a lot easier.

4. Becoming A Member of the C-Suite

Women everywhere are making positive changes in the workplace, and one of the greatest obstacles they face is advancing to C-suite level positions. Know what you want and be relentless in your pursuit to achieve your goal.

5. Overcoming Perfectionism

Many women leaders can get paralyzed by perfection syndrome. I recommend removing yourself from the situation and taking a mental break. It might be practicing meditation, an activity such as taking a walk, or journaling. These approaches have worked well to help manage and overcome perfectionism.

402.   Getting the Raise/Promotion You Deserve

Most people don't know how to ask for a promotion or raise. So, being well prepared to have the conversation can help reduce your anxiety and significantly increase the likelihood of getting what you want.

What Are Some Tips for Getting a Promotion or Raise?

Be Realistic

Before an employee can or should ask for a promotion or raise, they should do an honest evaluation of their performance over the previous year. In addition to being real about how you performed, it's a good idea to review the salary range for your position before you decide to ask for a promotion or raise. By providing your zip code and position title, a salary calculator will tell you what your salary range is for your area. This is useful information to have on hand as you prepare your thoughts.

Collect Your Evidence

A significant percentage of getting what you want, when you ask for a promotion or raise, is providing supporting documentation. Employees who have taken the time to collect evidence of their achievements, against the goals of the company, are more likely to get what they want. I also recommend keeping a digital file on your work computer to keep track of ideas, recognition, and achievements you've made with the company. That way, you have easy access to the information needed and you don't have to spend countless hours trying to think of what you did or where the information is located.

These employees are also more likely to advance into more senior roles and better salaries. The best conversations around pay increases and title changes happen when an employee can show how their performance positively affected productivity and profitability. Being able to show this demonstrates that an employee is invested both in their professional growth and in the success of their organization.

Practice Your Pitch and Anticipate Questions

The conversations in which you are asking for something almost always go better if you've rehearsed them in advance. Consider the possible responses that you'll get to each of your questions, and how you'll address those responses. After having played the part of a resistant boss, having the actual conversation will be significantly easier, and you'll have more confidence since you'll be able to anticipate their answers and know how to address them.

Ask in Advance

By the time your performance review comes around, decisions about whether you'll receive a raise or bonus have already been made. If you plan to ask for more than just a cost of living increase, you'll need to have the conversation before performance review discussions are scheduled. A simple Word document with your achievements and requests laid out should be enough. Be sure not to withhold any data that you feel could be beneficial. Most successful employees prepare not just a list of achievements but specific measurements of their performance.

Illuminate your Irreplaceability

Ask yourself what you do for your organization that no one else can do, but more importantly, come to the table with the right attitude. There is a fine line between being assertive and rude when making a request. Keeping your feelings in check before discussing advancement with your boss is critical, especially if you aren't a top performer. Being consistent throughout the year is also important, whether you ask for an increase or not. Ending every one-on-one meeting with your manager by asking: "What can I do better?" gives the impression that you're receptive to criticism. Remember that it's a two-way street and work needs to take place on your end also.

Regardless of how well you've done at work this year, there are always areas where you can improve your performance or stretch your goals. These personal performance goals should be a part of the raise/promotion conversation, even if you get what you want.

Play the Long Game

Ask, and you shall receive, doesn't always apply when it comes to raises and promotions. For a variety of reasons, you should always go into negotiations with the understanding that you won't always get what you want. Whether it's a matter of improving your performance or increasing your experience level, your manager may not be able to offer you exactly what you are asking for this year. They should, however, be able to offer you a plan for how to arrive at your desired destination. Be open to working with them on creating a timeline of tasks, goals, professional enrichment courses or whatever it will take to make you the most qualified, to earn the money you want, or gain the title you desire. The worst that can happen is that your boss says no. Either way, you'll learn to advocate for yourself and understand and appreciate your worth. Look at it this way; there's little chance you'll get more money if you never ask!

403. How to Start Your Own Business

With many people wanting to pursue entrepreneurship or create a side hustle to make extra money, it's easy to just want to jump into the process. However, there is a legal aspect of doing business that needs to take place. You don't want anyone else to capitalize on your success, but in the same vein, you wouldn't want to operate your business under the same name as anyone else in your area. That could lead to legal action, lawyers, and a hefty payout to the other party. With all there is to consider, it's best to create a business with your state government to ensure you and your assets are protected. While each state may vary slightly in the way they operate, below is a quick list of things you should consider. While an LLC is not right for every business, it's how a lot of small businesses get started. Take the time to research your particular industry or the goals you want for your company to decide which business structure works best for you. Remember in the end, the time you spend update can save you from a lot of headaches and heartbreaks down the road.

How to Start an LLC

- Choose a registered agent—a registered agent is a person who agrees to receive official documents on behalf of the LLC and to pass them along to the appropriate person at the LLC
- Prepare an LLC operating agreement—it specifies such things as the ownership interests and voting rights of the members, how profits and losses will be allocated, etc. Not required by all states.
- File organizational paperwork with the state—in general, you must file articles of the organization that list things such as the name and address of the LLC, the length of its existence, etc.
- Pay fee—there is a fee required by the state to register your business. Prices vary by state.
- Obtain a certificate from the state—this is available once registration is completed online.

- Register to do business in other states—mostly used if you're selling a product or service.
- Once officially registered, apply for EIN at IRS.GOV
- Open a business bank account—certain financial institutions offer specific benefits for opening a business account. Do some research before deciding who to bank with.
- Set up business email—This helps to separate yourself from the business and can help you to appear that you have a team behind you when you're first starting.
- Create website/social media pages—this helps to provide credibility for your business.
- Set up a payment system—having multiple forms of payment helps increase the likeliness of making a sale.
- THINK PROFESSIONALISM AT EVERY STEP—If you think like a business, you'll operate as a business!

Disclaimer: This list is not all-inclusive. Depending on your business or state in which you operate, this should serve as a guide.

404. Side Hustle Pro

Many of the most successful startups started as a side hustle. Even if your side hustle doesn't achieve runaway success, it is still a valuable experience. After all, it can be an opportunity to work on a personal passion or expand your network while bringing in a secondary revenue stream.

Separate your Work Self from your Personal Self

It is easy to get immersed in the daily grind of working a job every day, especially if you like the work you are doing. However, be careful with getting lost in another company and abandoning the desire to start your own. A side hustle isn't just a nice-to-have; it's critical, especially in this social climate. You might even discover that your side hustle improves your performance in your current role, and it provides you with a new set of skills. It's not about work-life balance. It's about creating an environment outside of your 9-to-5 and aligning yourself with what motivates you. Take time to reflect and ask yourself what would truly make you happy.

Establish Boundaries and Structure

A side hustle shouldn't interfere with your job performance, but it is important to establish boundaries. Commit to a scheduled time where you work on only your personal project. Don't check your work email during that time, and don't feel bad about skipping a non-essential work event if it interferes—set milestones for your project to stay on track. Align your milestones around key performance indicators like visitors, active users, monthly revenue, and other metrics aligned to your project.

Monetize Your Passion

What many people get wrong about a side hustle is that it isn't just about making extra money or pursuing a personal ambition. It has to be both. Don't look at a side hustle as a secondary revenue stream or a passion. Combine the two. Monetizing your side hustle allows you to pursue your passion while also offering a financial incentive. However unfamiliar your passion may currently be, be creative and find a path to make it profitable. Often, those are the businesses most profitable because they don't face any competition.

Surround Yourself with People Who Have Similar Passions

Taking on a side project may mean working extended hours on your own time. You might have to turn down social outings and weekend nights with friends to stay in and work. But don't shut people out completely. Try to find a person or group who share your similar interests. Social interaction is beneficial to your health and well-being. Having a group of people that shares your passion, that you can have fun with, can help inspire creativity and also be a soundboard when you need advice or things get rough.

Even if you can focus or work productively from home, it may be worthwhile to join a co-working space or work from a local coffee shop. Your network will open new opportunities for you and support you during the hard times that come with starting anything new. As long as your side hustle doesn't compete with your day job, go for it. A side hustle gives you perspective, enhances your professional skillset, offers secondary income, and provides an outlet for you to pursue a personal dream.

Keeps You Fresh and Improves Your Motivation

Having something else to occupy your mind doesn't just stop you from getting bored; it can also keep you fresh. You'll bring all of those new skills to your job, and you'll find ways to use them, even if it isn't always obvious. You'll push yourself, you'll try new things, and you'll adapt your style. This can help you to feel motivated at work again. You'll feel fresh. In this way, your side hustle can have a massive impact on your career.

You Could Make Important Connections with Your Side Hustle

A side hustle doesn't just give you a way to make money and develop new skills. It can also be a fantastic chance to meet new people and make new connections. Some of these connections might be useful at work, or they might give you opportunities in the future. Others might just become good friends who become part of your support network and offer you friendship, advice, and support whenever you need it. Your side hustle can lead to lifelong friendships and vital business connections.

BIBLE VERSES

Psalm 32:8
I will instruct you and teach you in the way you should go; I will counsel you with my eye upon you.

Proverbs 16:3
Commit your work to the Lord, and your plans will be established.

Ecclesiastes 9:10
Whatever your hand finds to do, do it with your might, for there is no work or thought or knowledge or wisdom in Sheol, to which you are going.

Romans 12:6-8
Having gifts that differ according to the grace given to us, let us use them: if prophecy, in proportion to our faith; if service, in our serving; the one who teaches, in his teaching; the one who exhorts, in his exhortation; the one who contributes, in generosity; the one who leads, with zeal; the one who does acts of mercy, with cheerfulness.

Ephesians 2:10
For we are his workmanship, created in Christ Jesus for good works, which God prepared beforehand, that we should walk in them.

Chapter 5
Authentically You

PRAYER FOR AUTHENTICITY

Father God,

Thank you that You so clearly spell out what an authentic Christian looks like. Please, help me to walk in the power of Your Holy Spirit. That is the only way I can even attempt to walk blamelessly and righteously. Help me today to speak truthfully in all things and to keep my mouth free from words that do not build others up. Help me to refrain from comments that cast a negative light on another. Father, help me to honor other believers even when I disagree with them. May I be a person of my word and generous in all my ways.

In Jesus' name I pray,
Amen.

501.   Let's Address our Mental Health

As a woman, it usually falls on your shoulders to be the caregiver and to make sure the needs of your family are met. This can be an exhausting and selfless job that doesn't receive nearly the credit that it deserves. You may put your needs behind those that you serve, and in return, not receive the care and attention you need. These feelings can lead to anxiety, depression, or several other mental illnesses. You have to make sure that you are also a priority in your life. Until you get to a place where you're able to pour into yourself, you're not going to be able to fully care and encourage the thoughts needed for you to heal.

Common Mental Illnesses

Depression

Depression is the most common mental disorder and generally affects women more often than men. It is often defined by loss of interest or pleasure, general sadness, feelings of guilt or low self-worth, difficulty falling asleep, eating pattern changes, exhaustion, and a lack of concentration. Several factors such as genetics, life events, medical problems, and medications can bring the illness on.

Because depression can present as long-lasting or recurring, it can severely interfere with a person's ability to function at work or school and harm relationships. At its most severe state, depression can lead to suicidal thoughts and actions.

Anxiety

It is not uncommon for a person experiencing depression to also have anxiety. It's incredibly common for anxiety to be coupled with depression, eating disorders, or addictive disorders like substance abuse.

Anxiety can develop from various factors, including genetics, brain chemistry, and life events, and while it is treatable, not many people who live with anxiety seek out treatment.

More "intense" anxiety disorders include panic disorder, post-traumatic stress disorder (PTSD), and phobias. Women are much more vulnerable to the development of most anxiety disorders than men.

Attention Deficit Hyperactivity Disorder (ADHD)

ADHD is a common mental disorder, but it's usually the most evident in preschools and elementary schools. However, some teenagers can develop ADHD as well. Interestingly, boys are more than twice likely to develop ADHD than girls. ADHD typically isn't harmful and can be very manageable.

Bipolar Affective Disorder

Engendering both manic and depressive episodes, sometimes book-ended, and sometimes featuring moments of "normal" or stabilized mood, this illness impacts approximately 60 million people worldwide. Manic episodes can contain elevated or irritable mood, hyperactivity, inflated self-esteem, and a lack of desire to sleep.

Hypomania is a less severe form of mania. Depressive episodes are often characterized by feelings of extreme sadness, hopelessness, little energy, and trouble sleeping.

Schizophrenia

Schizophrenia is characterized by distortions in thinking, perception, emotions, sense of self, and behavior. Those who have this illness can experience hallucinations and delusions starting in late adolescence or early adulthood, making it difficult for people to work, study, or interact socially.

Impulse Control Disorder

Impulse control disorders (also called addictive disorders) are ones in which people are mentally incapable of resisting impulses. The people who struggle with impulse control are likely to become so absorbed with the object(s) of their addiction that they start to neglect other areas of their life, such as responsibilities and relationships. This is especially harmful since poor impulse control can lead to other things like self-harm or harm to others. Substance abuse, gambling addiction, kleptomania, and even pyromania, are all common examples of impulse control disorders.

Mental health illnesses touch nearly every person in some way. While every situation is unique, there are treatment and recovery options available to help an individual or family member achieve strength and support. Taking the time to recognize symptoms and get an accurate diagnosis can help determine the most appropriate treatment.

502.   Pouring into Yourself

Let's be honest for a moment. There are times when, as hard as you work, things just don't go your way. You've done the research, you've been the bigger person, you've even helped contribute to the success of someone else, but you still didn't get what you wanted. Those moments in life will happen, and the last thing you want to hear is a pep talk. You just need to be in the moment, but it's in those times when God can do His best work. It's when lessons are learned that faith is activated, solutions are realized, and we choose to work harder.

So, when this happens to me, I make up my mind on how I want to move forward and get to work, but not without the little extra support from one of my favorite things or music. I created a Girl Power Playlist to act as my support system when I need to encourage myself. It gets me back in the right perspective and reminds me that "I got this; I can do this!"

My Girl Power Playlist

- Beyoncé - Run the world
- Ciara - Level Up
- Ariana Grande - Dangerous Woman
- Katy Perry - Roar
- Destiny's Child - Survivor
- Alicia Keys - Girl on Fire
- Miley Cyrus - Wrecking Ball
- Beyoncé - Diva
- Fifth Harmony - Worth It
- Demi Lovato - Sorry not Sorry
- Iggy Azalea - Black Widow
- Fifth Harmony - Bo$$
- Demi Lovato - Confident
- Whitney Houston - I'm every Woman
- Destiny's Child - Independent Women
- Ariana Grande – God is a Woman
- Fergie - MILF $
- Jennifer Lopez -Dinero
- Rihanna - Hard
- Nicki Minaj - Feeling Myself
- Lizzo - Good as Hell
- Shania Twain - Man! I feel like a Woman
- Keri Hilson - Pretty Girl Rock
- Little Mix - Power
- Gwen Stefani - Hollaback Girl

503. Being True to Who You Are

Being true to who you are means you don't worry about pleasing other people or living by someone else's standards. You don't care what people think, but you trust where God is leading you. You live as your authentic self, without compromise, and building a life you desire.

You're Connected to the Holy Spirit

You've been able to clear your mind off constant distractions to hear from the Holy Spirit. You can allow the Holy Spirit to guide your actions with trust and faith.

You Are Willing to See and Acknowledge Your Faults

You don't judge others for their prejudices, but you see it as a part of the person's hurt that is yet to heal. You know that there are aspects of yourself that you don't like, and you're willing to do the necessary work required to heal from past traumas.

You Take Responsibility for Your Life

You don't blame other people for what happens in your life. You take personal responsibility for how your actions created a certain outcome. You are willing to look at how you influenced each situation and act accordingly.

You Recognize That Experiences Make Your Life Richer

You're aware of how life experiences create more meaning and richness in your life. You are open to explore and learn, both externally and internally.

You Truly Listen to Others

You're able to be fully present with another person. You're able to listen to others with genuine interest and care for the other person.

You Express Your True Thoughts, Feelings, and Views Unapologetically

You don't say things that you don't truly mean. You don't do things that you don't want to do. You can share your unique thoughts, feelings, and views without fear of other's opinions.

You're Not Out to Please People

You know the importance of being aware, acknowledging, and expressing your unique thoughts, feelings, and views of the world. You know that by expressing your experience, you can share your gifts with the world.

You See Value in Giving Love to Others

You see value in giving love and kindness to everyone. You understand that we are all connected and are willing to give others a helping hand. You allow and encourage others to express their truth with love and acceptance as well.

You Love Yourself

You see yourself as a person of value who deserves love, kindness, and support. You provide yourself with adequate care to support your health and well-being.

You Understand That We Are All Unique

You know that not everyone is going to agree on everything all the time. You are accepting of differing views and opinions.

504. Self-Love

Self-love is the foundation for being able to truly and selflessly love and show love to others. Without loving yourself, it is hard to be completely selfless in a relationship with anyone. It's important because it is from this space that all good relationships with others are formed. It's so easy to focus on your faults and insecurities instead of what makes you happy. This can ultimately hinder your journey to self-discovery, purpose, and healing.

Why It's Important to Love Yourself

Being in love with yourself provides you with self-confidence and self-worth, and it will generally help you feel more positive. You may also find that it is easier for you to fall in love once you have learned to love yourself first. If you can learn to love yourself, you will be much happier and learn how to best take care of yourself. When you are truly in love with yourself and happy, you should stop comparing yourself to others so much and should find yourself more confident, not worrying as much about what others think.

How to Love Yourself: Self-Love Tips

It's good to find the best ways for you personally to love yourself, as you will most likely learn new things about yourself and start trying new things in the process.

Some of these steps may seem scary at first, but once you have mastered the ways that work for you, you will feel so much happier and can truly say that you love yourself. Here are some self-love tips you can try today to discover how to love yourself and own your confidence!

Have Fun by Yourself

It's always good to have a few days set aside for yourself, that is just for you to do something fun. In doing this, you can learn to enjoy your own company, and most likely feel more confident doing it on your own. This could include going to the movies, having dinner at a nice restaurant, or finding new things to try.

Travel Once A Year

This may be completely out of your comfort zone, but that is a good thing! If you can travel on your own, this will be a great self-love experience. You will be learning new things not only about yourself but also about another culture. This also helps to bring you out of your normal routine.

Surprise Yourself

Try things out of your control and say yes to things you would not normally say yes to. This will also help you with getting to know yourself. You may find out that you enjoy things you never realized or tried before. Try and get out of your comfort zone and see what happens.

Start a Journal

If you can write down your thoughts and feelings, you can go back later and see how you coped with certain situations. This is also a positive way for you to get rid of any negative experiences and feelings, thereby helping you to focus on the good things and learn from the bad.

Say No to Others

Sometimes, we do too much for people. We like to please other people, so we tend to stretch ourselves too thin and commit to everything we can. We can forget to look after ourselves sometimes, so that's why it is good to say no. Focus on yourself when you can, or if you are overwhelmed.

List Your Accomplishments

Creating a list of what you have achieved is a great way to fall in love with yourself. This makes you feel good about yourself and find happiness from what you have accomplished. We can sometimes focus on the negatives and forget about the positives, so this is a great way to remind yourself of what you have achieved.

Pursue New Interests

It's great to try something new that you have wanted to try for a while or have been too scared to do. You never know what you might enjoy until you try it, so think of a new hobby you could try, or go to a place you've wanted to go to for a while.

Challenge Yourself

If you can challenge yourself, you will also be getting to know yourself and what you are capable of. Just go for it and see what happens.

Work on Your Self-Trust

A great way to show yourself self-love is to trust yourself and your own instincts. You are most likely going to know what is best for you, and self-trust is a step to self-love. You need to trust yourself before you can trust others, so listen to your gut and trust how you feel.

BIBLE VERSES:

Isaiah 58:11
The Lord will guide you continually, watering your life when you are dry and keeping healthy, too. You will be like an ever-flowing spring.

Proverbs 17:22
A cheerful heart does good like medicine, but a broken spirit makes one sick.

2 Timothy 2:15
Do your best to present yourself to God as one approved, a worker who has no need to be ashamed, rightly handling the word of truth.

John 17:26
I made known to them your name, and I will continue to make it known, that the love with which you have loved me may be in them, and I in them.

James 5:12
But above all, my brothers, do not swear, either by heaven or by earth or by any other oath, but let your "yes" be yes and your "no" be no, so that you may not fall under condemnation.

Chapter 6
Facing Your Finances

PRAYER FOR FINANCES

Dear Heavenly Father,

I come to you with a heart full of thanksgiving and recognizing that every good gift and every perfect gift is from You. I pray for a spirit of self-discipline as I deal with money, wealth, my daily living habits, and my pleasures. Help me to do all in moderation and according to your will. I ask that You place Your hand on my finances and open my heart to receive new mercies. I trust in Your ability to prosper me in this time. I pray that there will be an overflow released from the north, south, east, and west. Father, grab hold of my life and teach me to prosper in this season. Holy Spirit bless the fruit of my hands, heart and mind, that I will be able to find opportunities to prosper in this season.

In Jesus' name
Amen.

601. The Basics of Credit

Credit is part of your financial power. Often, the hardest part about the credit process is the reality of where you're starting. A lot of people experience highs and lows when it comes to their credit journey. The important concept to remember is that, like most things, you must learn how to be successful. You must educate yourself on the fundamentals of credit and build your expertise from there.

Getting Started

There are three credit-reporting bureaus: Experian, Equifax, and TransUnion. The credit bureaus keep track of your credit history, which is attached to your SSN. This is what creditors use to determine how much of a risk you'll be when asking for a loan. Based on your history, they each assign you a value, based on your history called a credit score. Since these are separate agencies, the score is most likely different across each of their platforms. That's why it's important to look at each of them when reviewing your credit report. Credit scores will range from 300-850.

Credit Reports

It's important to pull your full credit report at least once a year. Checking your own score won't hurt you, and each bureau offers individuals a free, detailed copy of your credit report each year. You can access a copy from the link provided https://www.annualcreditreport.com/index.action. Once you download the copy, you may save it to your computer. Otherwise, you may have to pay for another copy.

Credit Resources

- Credit Karma - https://www.creditkarma.com/about

    Credit Karma offers free monthly credit scores. They keep you updated and allow you to dispute inaccuracies directly from their website.

- Discover IT - https://creditscorecard.com

    The Discover Scorecard provides monthly updates to your credit score. It alerts you to any unusual activity, new accounts opened in your name, and provides a breakdown of your credit history so you know what improvements you can make.

- Lender - https://www.self.inc/

    An opportunity to build credit monthly by putting your money away into a separate account. It's a loan that also helps you save money. At the end of the designated time, they can send you a check which you can use to pay off a bill, save for an emergency, or take a trip. The possibilities are endless. Who doesn't want to save a couple of dollars? I know I do!

- Magnify Money - http://www.magnifymoney.com/

    Gives honest reviews of credit cards

- Credit Sesame - https://creditsesame.go2cloud.org/aff_c?offer_id=38&aff_id=441

A free credit monitoring tool that gives you your credit score & report for free as well as up to $50,000 in identity theft insurance for FREE!

Building your Credit

If you're looking to build or even repair your credit, the resources provided are great places to start. Most of them allow you to monitor your credit score for free, every month. Websites such as Credit Karma will allow you to dispute your credit report directly from their website. When going through this process, it's important to pay close attention to your credit reports and dispute any inaccuracies, especially if you're looking to make a large purchase in the near future. These purchases can include buying a car, home, or can even affect employment. Paying your bills on time and using less than 30% of your available credit limits (the lower the better) will help in building a strong score.

Credit Education

While there are many companies out there that will do the repair work for you, they can also come with some pretty hefty prices. If that's something you can't afford or want to do it yourself, it doesn't have to be a painful process. The biggest hurdle is knowing where to look to get reliable advice. Aside from the resources I am providing, a lot of information can be found online through Facebook and Podcasts. I think Podcasts are one of the best options because you can subscribe to specific stations that are vital to you, without having to spend time searching through articles. They also provide guidance in quickly paying off loans you already have and prepare you to buy a house or give you general credit tips.

602.   How to Dispute your Credit Report

Now that you've had an opportunity to become familiar with your credit reports, let's talk about getting negative remarks removed from your credit profile and increasing your credit score. A lot of times, the credit bureaus receive your personal information second hand. This can happen when you apply for a loan, complete an application, or change addresses. Thus, some of the information they have may be incorrect, most often due to human error. They may misread your information or key in the wrong numbers, and those errors can hurt your credit score. That's why it's important to stay on top of your information so that you don't end up literally paying more in the long run.

If you do happen to find incorrect information on your credit report or want to remove negative remarks, the tips below can help:

Step 1: DISPUTE, DISPUTE, DISPUTE

Keep in mind that the reporting agencies update once a month, so it may take a month or two before you start seeing an increase in your credit score.

Step 2: WRITE A LETTER

When a bureau reports a negative inquiry (late payment, non-payment, etc.), it can have a huge impact on your credit score. One of the ways to try and have the information removed is to write the company or bureau a letter.

Here are some resources available by a quick internet search or entering the links below to get you started. (Note: You may have to send a letter to each of the agencies to request the removal of the information).

- Cease & Desist Letter Templates: http://thebudgetnistablog.com/2015/stop-calls/
- Debt Verification/Validation Letter Templates: https://www.ovlg.com/letters/debt-verification-letter.html
- Dispute Letter Template: http://thebudgetnistablog.com/2015/credit-clean/
- Inquiry Removal Letter Template: https://aaacreditguide.com/credit-inquiry-removal-letter/
- Use a Goodwill Letter to Remove Late Payments from Your Credit Report: https://twocents.lifehacker.com/use-a-goodwill-letter-to-remove-late-payments-from-your-1680276221
- Pay for Delete Letter: https://www.crediful.com/pay-for-delete-letter/
- Letter to get car repossession off your credit report: https://aaacreditguide.com/repossessions/
- Vehicle Repossession Letter: Use this repossession letter to dispute collection activity:

https://www.creditinfocenter.com/forms/sampleletter18. shtml
- How to dispute child support on your credit report: http://info.legalzoom.com/dispute-child-support-reporting-credit-report-22980.html
- How to File a Satisfaction of Judgment: Creditors must follow through on this important step after a judgment debt has been paid off. https://www.nolo.com/legal-encyclopedia/free-books/small-claims-book/chapter23-3.html
- FREE Credit Letters: A bunch of free credit letters: http://www.creditservicer.com/pages/credit-repair/free-sample-letters.php

Step 3: KEEP UP THE GOOD WORK

As you've probably noticed, the efforts to bring up your credit score can be a long and hard process that often can take months and sometimes years, to really see. Once you've raised your credit score, you can start to experience new opportunities. You will find it easier to get financing; your interest rates will decrease, and it may eliminate you having to put money down for larger purchases. With all of the hard work you put in, you will want to continue to maintain your credit score for the long term. Although you may no longer see the same sharp increase in your credit score as you did in the beginning, you'll want to make sure you don't compromise all the work you initially did. And if you find yourself in a similar situation again, rest assured that you now know what it takes to improve.

603.   The Burden of Student Loans

One of the biggest myths I've heard when it comes to student loans is that if you have them, then you can't purchase a house, which is absolutely not true. I bought my first home/property with over $50,000 in student loan debt, at the time. But depending on the amount of your student loans and your annual income, you may not qualify for a loan. There are two things you must be mindful of during the home-buying process. One, your student loans can't be in default and expect to get a home loan. Secondly, the amount owned does go against your debt-income ratio, which banks use to determine the purchase amount of the home you intend to buy. So, if you have the option to pay down or pay off your student loans, then that will always be your best option.

Tips to Pay off your Loans

By now, you've probably noticed that I LOVE to provide tips and tricks I tried throughout my journey. This one comes in the form of an app called ChangEd. I'm in love with this app because it allows me to round up every purchase I make on my debit card to the nearest dollar. After $5 or more, they transfer the money from my bank account and put it towards my student loan. Once you reach $100, they make a payment onto your student loan account. You also have the option to designate $5, $10, or $20 from your account at any time. So, if you have a little bit of extra money at the end of the week, then you can transfer that amount from your account and put it towards your student loans. Any time you log into the app, you can see at a glance the average number of days it takes for you to make a $100 payment, how far away you are from having money deducted from your account, etc. They've also partnered with SoFi, a company that offers to consolidate or refinance student loans, which you may access also.

Employee Tuition Assistance Programs

Working in HR for most of my career, I also know that employees who take advantage of their tuition reimbursement program often go unutilized. This program is typically available for employees currently enrolled in college courses. There are usually stipulations around using this resource such as the program has to benefit your current role or team. It may require you to sign a time commitment with your company or you would be asked to pay back the money they offered. For example, if your company helped pay for two years of your education, they may request that you stay on with the company for two years after graduating. As a business, they want to ensure they are investing in associates who are also invested in the organization. This could potentially save you $10,000 in loans that you would be responsible for paying back later. Now, I understand that every organization and situation is different; however, it is important to consider all your options when taking on a huge debt like student loans and saving yourself the burden of dealing with repayment later in life.

Assistance Based on Profession

There are also options for student loan forgiveness, depending on your profession. If you're fairly new to college and still deciding between majors, or if you're in these professions or companies, this is something to keep in mind:

Companies that pay off student loans

1. **Aetna:** Aetna is a health insurance provider that gives its full-time employees up to $2,000 per year for their student loans with a $10,000-lifetime limit. Part-time employees working 20 or more hours per week are eligible for $1,000 per year with a $5,000-lifetime limit. You must have earned your degree within three years of applying to qualify.

2. **Carhartt:** Clothing retailer, Carhartt, offers qualifying full and part-time employees $50 per month toward their student loans with a maximum $10,000-lifetime benefit. Nonunion members are eligible for student loan repayment assistance after 30 days of employment, while union members must wait until they've worked for the company for 90 days.

3. **Carvana:** Car-buying platform, Carvana, has partnered with Gradifi, a startup that helps employers set up student loan repayment and assistance benefits, to offer their full-time employees $1,000 per year toward their student debt.

4. **Chegg:** This education technology company offers employees with student debt, $1,000 per year, with no lifetime maximum. Its Equity for Education program gives employees in entry-to-manager-level jobs an additional $5,000 annually for student debt. Employees need to be with the company for two years to qualify. Directors and vice presidents are eligible for an additional $3,000 annually under this program.

5. **CommonBond:** CommonBond, a student loan refinancing marketplace, offers employees $100 per month toward their student loans until all of their loans are paid off.

6. **Estee Lauder:** Employees of Estee Lauder and its subsidiaries, including Clinique, MAC Cosmetics, and Origins, are eligible for a $100 monthly student loan repayment benefit. The company caps the lifetime benefit at $10,000.

7. **Fidelity Investments:** Fidelity's Step Ahead Student Loan Assistance Program offers employees who have been with the company for, at least, six months up to $2,000 per year for their student loans with a maximum $10,000-lifetime benefit.

8. **Gradifi:** Gradifi helps other companies establish student loan repayment and employee benefits. It offers $250 per month, up to $10,000 in total.

9. **Honeywell:** Honeywell has also partnered with Gradifi to offer up to $10,000 in student loan repayment assistance to qualifying employees. It pays $150 per month.

10. **Hulu:** Employees of the popular streaming service carrying student loan debt can expect to receive $1,200 per year toward their student loans.

11. **LendEDU:** Online loan marketplace LendEDU offers employees $200 per month toward student loan repayment with no maximum cap.

12. **Live Nation:** Entertainment company Live Nation matches employee student loan payments up to $100 per month with a $6,000-lifetime maximum. Employees must be with the company for at least six months to qualify.

13. **Natixis Global Asset Management:** This company offers employees $1,000 per year in student loan repayment assistance with a maximum lifetime benefit of $10,000.

14. **Nvidia:** Tech company, Nvidia, offers full and part-time employees working at least 20 hours per week and $500 per month toward their student loans with a $30,000-lifetime maximum. Employees must work for the company, at least, three months before they qualify.

15. **Peloton:** Fitness company, Peloton, partnered with Gradifi in 2017, to offer its employees $100 per month in student loan repayment assistance.

16. **Penguin Random House:** This book publisher offers employees $100 per month in student loan repayment assistance with a maximum lifetime benefit of $9,000.

Only full-time employees that have been with the company for at least one year are eligible.

17. **PricewaterhouseCoopers:** Professional services company, PricewaterhouseCoopers (PwC), offers employees up to $1,200 per year in student loan repayment assistance with a $10,000 maximum lifetime benefit.

18. **SoFi:** The online lender offers employees up to $200 per month in student loan repayment assistance with no lifetime caps.

19. **Staples:** Staples offers qualifying, high-potential employees $100 per month in student loan repayment assistance for a maximum of 36 months.

20. **U.S. Government:** In addition to its Public Service Loan Forgiveness (PSLF), teacher loan forgiveness, and military loan forgiveness programs, the federal government offers employees up to $60,000 in student loan repayment assistance. This is paid in $10,000 increments over six years. Only federal student loans are eligible, and you must sign a contract agreeing to work for the government, for at least, three years.

604.   Homeownership

There are a lot of great programs out there to help those interested in owning a home. I want to briefly discuss some of those options available. If you have the opportunity, a first-time home-buying program is a great place to start. These programs are often hosted by a bank or accessible through a city program. They offer advice on credit building and repair, savings, the cost of owning a home, and much more. One of the biggest reasons people tend to go through these programs, aside from education, is that they usually can offer down payment or closing assistance. This means that you have to pay less out of your pocket, and I've even heard of people not having to pay anything, eventually ending up with a refund. Either way, owning a home is probably one of the biggest purchases you will ever make, so the more you know, the better.

Common Mortgage Loans

Conventional - This is a mortgage made by a bank to a buyer with no third party involved.

Pros

- Lower monthly mortgage insurance, making the overall monthly payment lower
- No mortgage insurance needed if 20% down
- If mortgage insurance is needed, it can go away once the buyer has 20% in equity
- Property standards not as picky
- Less paperwork involved

Cons

- Holds the buyer to a higher standard in terms of credit, savings, and debt-to-income ratio
- Larger down payment needed (5% minimum)
- Interest rate and monthly mortgage insurance is more expensive with lower credit scores

FHA - Loans insured by the Federal Housing Administration (part of HUD)

Pros

- More flexibility with newer and not perfect credit, limited savings, or tighter debt-to-income ratio.
- Down payment can be gifted from a family member.
- The interest rate is often lower than that of a conventional loan.
- Lower minimal down payment is needed than with a conventional loan (3.5% vs 5%).

Cons

- Monthly mortgage insurance is typically more expensive, and it stays for the life of the loan.
- The property needs to meet a higher standard inspection than needed for conventional loans.
- More paperwork is involved.

203(K) – FHA's 203(k) program permits homebuyers and homeowners to finance up to $35,000 into their mortgage to repair, improve, or upgrade their homes. They can tap into cash to pay for property repairs or improvements, such as those identified by a home inspector or an FHA appraiser. Homeowners can make property repairs, improvements, or prepare their home for sale.

They can also make their new home move-in ready by remodeling the kitchen, painting the interior, or purchasing new carpet.

VA - loans that are guaranteed by the Department of Veteran Affairs for eligible veterans

Pros

- No down payment is needed.
- No monthly mortgage insurance.
- VA funding fee can be waived if the Veteran has over 10% disability.
- The interest rate is often lower than for a conventional loan.

Cons

- Property needs to meet a higher standard of inspection.
- The seller has to pay for certain fees that are typically paid for by the buyer (ex. Closing fees).
- More paperwork is involved.

USDA - loans that are guaranteed for homes in areas deemed rural

Pros

- No down payment needed
- Monthly mortgage insurance is less expensive, making the overall payment lower
- In some situations, the cost of repairs can be rolled into the loan
- Interest rate is often lower than that of a conventional loan

Cons

- Only homes in eligible areas can be financed with USDA mortgages
- USDA needs to review all files, which often delays the closing process
- The home needs to meet minimum property standards set by USDA that are more stringent than some other loan types

While there may be other loans available to purchase a home, these are some of the most common. Ensure that whoever you're working with, whether an agent or broker, is familiar with the rules and regulations for the type of loan and property you are looking to purchase. You don't want to find a place that you love, have your offer accepted, and find out afterward that you need to put down a larger percentage or that your mortgage payments would be over $100 more than anticipated.

BIBLE VERSES

Matthew 6:21
For where your treasure is, there your heart will be also.

Romans 13:8
Owe no one anything, except to love each other, for the one who loves another has fulfilled the law.

Psalm 37:16-17
Better is the little that the righteous has than the abundance of many wicked. For the arms of the wicked shall be broken, but the Lord upholds the righteous.

Proverbs 13:11
Wealth gained hastily will dwindle, but whoever gathers little by little will increase it.

1 Timothy 6:17-19
As for the rich in this present age, charge them not to be haughty, nor to set their hopes on the uncertainty of riches, but on God, who richly provides us with everything to enjoy. They are to do good, to be rich in good works, to be generous and ready to share, thus storing up treasure for themselves as a good foundation for the future, so that they may take hold of that which is truly life.

Wrap Up

Now that you've had an opportunity to go through the chapters and each section, you should feel very proud of your progress. I know that this can be a long and intense journey. Taking a look at and revealing inner wounds is never an easy process. What did God reveal to you? Are there certain aspects of this book that you felt convicted of? Is there anything that you still need to work on? What steps do you have in place to help you stay committed?

In the next phase of your journey, these are the types of questions you should be asking yourself. They can also show you how far you've come and what you still need to accomplish. Take some time and meditate on what the next steps in your journey will look like. Do you need to spend some time repairing old relationships? Are you ready to start that business? Or do you need to work on your finances? Remember that the journey doesn't stop today. It only stops when you stop.

Stay tuned for the accompanying workbook to assist you in where you go from here.

REFERENCES

https://www.psychologytoday.com/us/blog/skinny-revisited/201805/self-care-101

http://trauma-recovery.ca/introduction/definition-of-trauma/

https://journeypureriver.com/big-t-little-t-trauma/

https://www.verywellmind.com/common-symptoms-after-a-traumatic-event-2797496

https://www.fool.com/student-loans/20-companies-pay-off-employees-student-loans/

https://www.businessnewsdaily.com/5489-female-leadership-advice.html

https://www.forbes.com/sites/forbescoachescouncil/2018/02/26/15-biggest-challenges-women-leaders-face-and-how-to-overcome-them/#3a7f7d254162

https://www.livecareer.com/resources/jobs/offers/how-to-ask-for-a-promotion-or-raise

https://www.forbes.com/sites/elanagross/2016/06/27/8-managers-share-the-best-way-to-ask-for-a-raise-and-get-it/#27408e1174ff

https://www.forbes.com/sites/paulinaguditch/2017/04/19/four-essential-strategies-for-launching-a-side-hustle-from-creative-leader-greg-wacks/#7af4380640f6

https://inspiretothrive.com/how-a-side-hustle-could-have-a-massive-impact-on-your-career/

https://www.hud.gov/program_offices/housing/sfh/203k

https://www.fromhispresence.com/how-to-break-unholy-soul-ties/

http://www.ministeringdeliverance.com/breaking_soul_ties.php

https://upliftconnect.com/why-you-should-forgive-your-parents-and-how-to-do-it/

https://www.healthline.com/health/how-to-forgive-yourself#7

https://www.biblestudytools.com/topical-verses/bible-verses-about-forgiving-yourself/

http://jameslau88.com/what_does_it_mean_to_be_made_whole.html

https://www.openbible.info/topics/made_whole

https://ineedyoujesusblog.wordpress.com/2018/02/15/to-have-a-servant-heart/

https://www.thenivbible.com/blog/10-biblical-purposes-fasting/

http://fastingforgod.org/purpose-of-fasting/

https://www.jackcanfield.com/blog/finding-life-purpose/

https://www.thebalancecareers.com/top-skills-every-professional-needs-to-have-4150386

https://www.ivyexec.com/career-advice/2019/mentor-versus-sponsor-differences-and-how-to-find/

https://www.verywellmind.com/tips-for-finding-your-purpose-in-life-4164689

https://www.huffpost.com/entry/11-signs-of-a-truly-authentic-person_b_9462220

https://www.thelawofattraction.com/love-yourself/

https://danwaldschmidt.com/11-ways-to-know-when-youve-found-your-purpose/